This igloo book belongs to:

....

igloobooks

Published in 2017
by Igloo Books Ltd
Cottage Farm
Sywell
NN6 0BJ
www.igloobooks.com

Copyright© 2014 Igloo Books Ltd

REX001 0117
4 6 8 10 9 7 5 3
ISBN 978-1-78440-212-9

Printed and manufactured in China

Grandma
Loves
Me

igloobooks

This is my grandma and this is me. I love my grandma because we have so much fun together.

When I go to visit Grandma, I run up the path to her house
and she scoops me up for a big, cuddly hug.

Grandma always joins in with my games,
dressing up and playing make-believe.

She pretends to be my fairy godmother, waving her wand with
a swish while I ride round on my magical pony.

When we bake cupcakes, my grandma lets me lick the bowl and doesn't mind when I get covered in sticky, pink frosting.

When the cupcakes are ready, Grandma shakes lots of sprinkles on top and they look so yummy, I can't wait to eat them!

I love to explore with my grandma. She teaches me the names of all the flowers and we pick the prettiest ones to take home.

Sometimes, I make a daisy chain for my grandma.

"I love it," she says with a big smile.

When I get wet in the rain, Grandma wraps me up with a lovely, snuggly blanket and gives me a hug and a kiss.

Grandma makes a hot drink to help me warm up, with fluffy
pink marshmallows floating on the top.

If it's too cold to play outside,
my grandma puts on some music.

We hold hands and dance around the
kitchen, spinning in circles
and laughing.

Then, we snuggle up in a comfy chair and Grandma shows me photos of when she was small and danced around the kitchen with her grandma.

When my grandma knits, her needles go Click! Clack! Click!
She has a basket full of wool, as bright as a rainbow.

Grandma is always making me jumpers, hats, mittens, socks and scarves too big for me.

I like to make things for my grandma, too. I paint pictures of us together with my best paints and cover them in sparkly glitter.

Grandma always loves the pictures that I give her and hangs them on the wall in her kitchen so she can look at them each day.

Grandma always reads me a story before I go to sleep at night.
She uses lots of different voices that make me giggle.

My grandma tucks me up with her best soft,
pink quilt to keep me cosy and warm.

When I go home the next morning, my grandma always gives me a little present to take with me.

I miss my grandma very much when we have to say goodbye,
but I know I'll see her again soon and I can't wait.

I love my grandma and I know she loves me too,
because that's what grandmas do best.